High in the tallest mountains of the world lies
the Mergich Realm, a sacred place of magic
and mystery where pure and powerful beings,
Mergichans, dwell. Guardian spirits, they tend
their flocks of mountain sheep and ibex,
and care for the sacred land. People enter
the Mergich Realm only with their permission.
They take the shape of an animal and this
is the story of one such Mergichan.

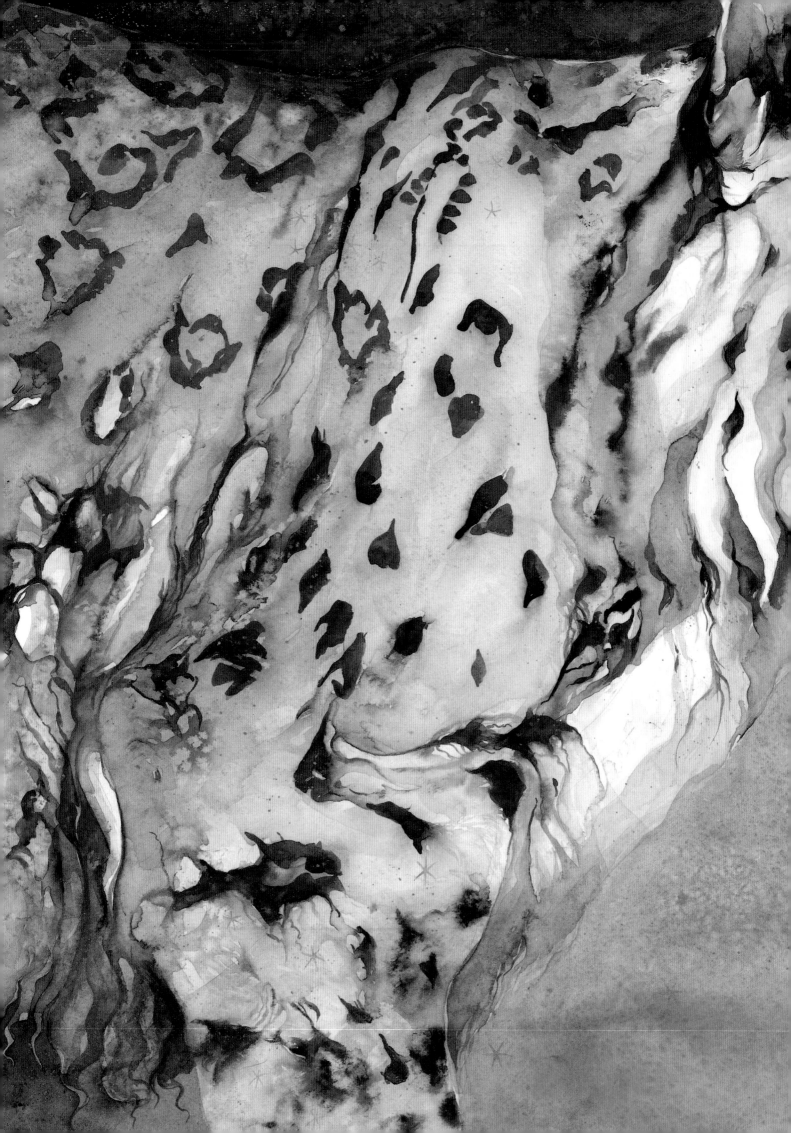

THE
SNOW LEOPARD

Jackie Morris

F

FRANCES LINCOLN
CHILDREN'S BOOKS

From the beginning of time, out of the silence,
Snow Leopard sang the stars to life, the sun to rise
and the moon to wax and wane. High above the hidden
valley, her song clothed the world in white and built
a crackling fortress of snow, buttressed with ice,
to keep all things safe and secret.

High in the mountains the sacred cat walked alone,
cloaked in her shadow-dappled fur. Crisp snow sparkled
in icy stars beneath her huge paws, and all the while she sang.
    Down in the valley the Child slept, and in her dreams
she heard the ghost cat's secret music and saw
the shadow of her dappled coat.

Snow Leopard wove words of protection, songs of hiding, a magic spell to keep the hidden valley safe from the world.

But time was passing, season upon season – and age creeps over all in time. So Snow Leopard changed her song to a spell of finding. She searched in her heart and called to find the next singer, the one who would come after her.

But while she searched, the world crept into the hidden valley.

And down in the valley the Child slept on and felt the change in the Snow Leopard's song.

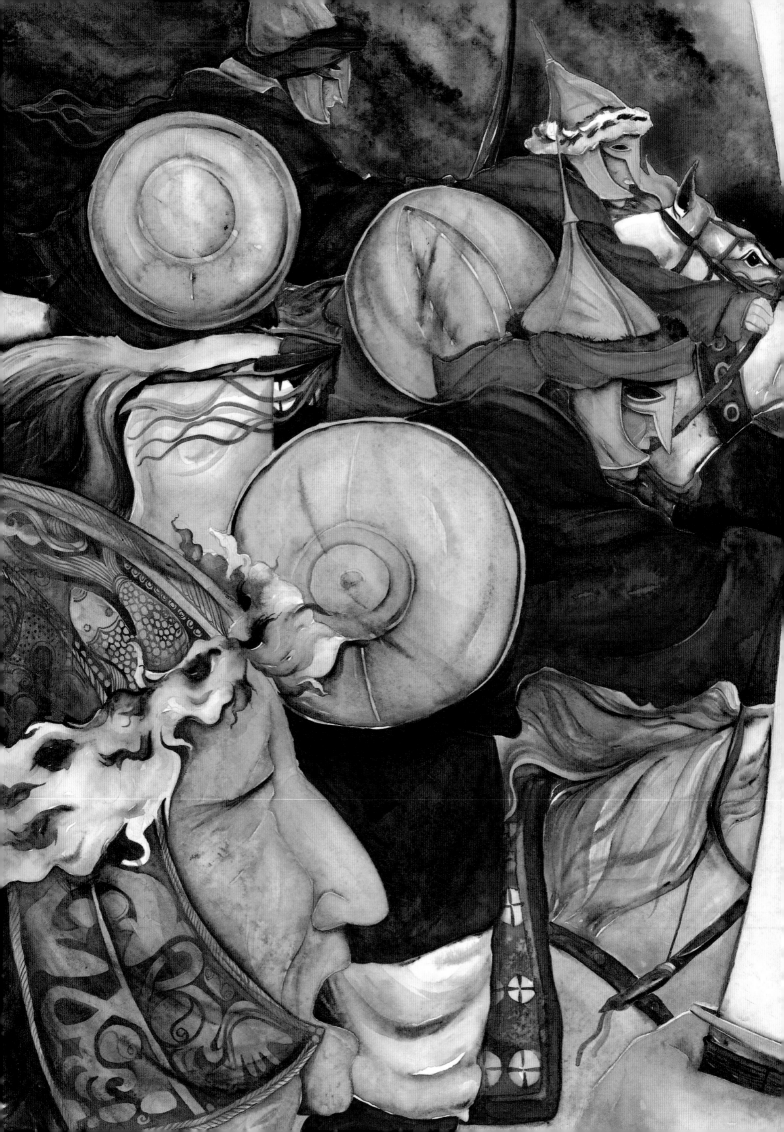

Down in the valley soldiers came,
in search of gold and slaves.
They came with fire and fear,
and the villagers fled.

In the chaos the sleeping girl
was forgotten. And still she slept,
entranced, hearing only the song
of the great ghost cat.

Through the village Snow Leopard prowled, veiled in the magic of her song. When she found the sleeping Child, she wrapped her warmly in her thick, dappled fur.

Curled around the Child, Snow Leopard remembered, centuries before, being human.

The sleeping Child woke feeling the warm breath
of the spirit cat close on her skin, wrapped in the fur
of the Snow Leopard, the singing cat of her dreams.
   She pushed her fingers deep into the thick fur
and the cat stirred, rose and leapt up to the high,
wild mountains with the Child clinging
tight on her back.

Together they roamed the mountain-tops and together they walked through the forests, and Snow Leopard sang her songs of the earth.

She taught the Child songs of the valley, of the lark and the swift, the snowfinch and redstart. She showed her the paths of the sure-footed fox and the scrape where the hare hid hushed in the snow.

She sang a song to protect the valley, to call the snow and ice, and the Child's voice joined in harmony as she listened and learned and they circled the valley, singing their song together.

Late in the night, while the soldiers were sleeping,
the stealthy cat crept back to the village, and into their
dreams. Snow Leopard raged, not one cat, but many,
a snowstorm of leopards. As their dreams became
nightmares the soldiers woke and ran from the village
they thought haunted by demons.

Hearing the news that the soldiers had gone,
the villagers returned with their prayer flags and lullabies
to blow in the wind and bring peace to the valley.
And circling the valley, Child and Leopard called to
the snow and a blizzard of white formed
fresh fortress walls, hiding their
world in mist and in memory.

Time passed, and the Child learned the moods of the valley, how to still her mind and become one with the place, how to ride on the thermals with eagle and falcon, to watch for the moon bear, bharal and wolf.

Snow Leopard purred richly at these changes. Her teaching finished, her time changed too.

Late one evening, in a cave of soft mosses high in the mountains
where the air was thin and stars sparkled in sky and snow,
the Child took the great leopard's head in her hands.

   The Snow Leopard licked the Child's cold face,
rough cat tongue against soft skin, purring
her final spirit song. And as she licked,
Child became Leopard, thick-furred
and wild-eyed, mottled like shadows,
spirit cat.

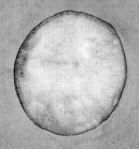

As the old Leopard finished her song she leapt
from the mountain into the star-filled sky,
her dappled coat blending with the stars of the Milky Way,
and her song changed to a whisper of starlight.

And back in the mountains,
the young Snow Leopard looked up
at the stars mirrored in her blue cat's eyes,
heard the whisper –
and began a new song.

*To Vivian French, for her encouragement and friendship,
to snow leopards in the high, wild mountains of the world,
and to my children, in the hope that when they are grown
snow leopards will still prowl in the Merghic Realms.*

The Snow Leopard copyright © Frances Lincoln Limited 2007
Text and illustrations copyright © Jackie Morris 2007

First published in Great Britain and the USA in 2007 by
Frances Lincoln Children's Books, 4 Torriano Mews,
Torriano Avenue, London NW5 2RZ
www.franceslincoln.com

Distributed in the USA by Publishers Group West

British Library Cataloguing in Publication Data
available on request

ISBN 978-1-84507-600-9

Illustrated with watercolours

Set in Centaur MT

Printed in China
9 8 7 6 5 4 3 2 1

**Visit Jackie Morris's website at
www.jackiemorris.co.uk**